Witches
and
fairies

Written
and illustrated by

Eva Montanari

meadowside
CHILDREN'S BOOKS

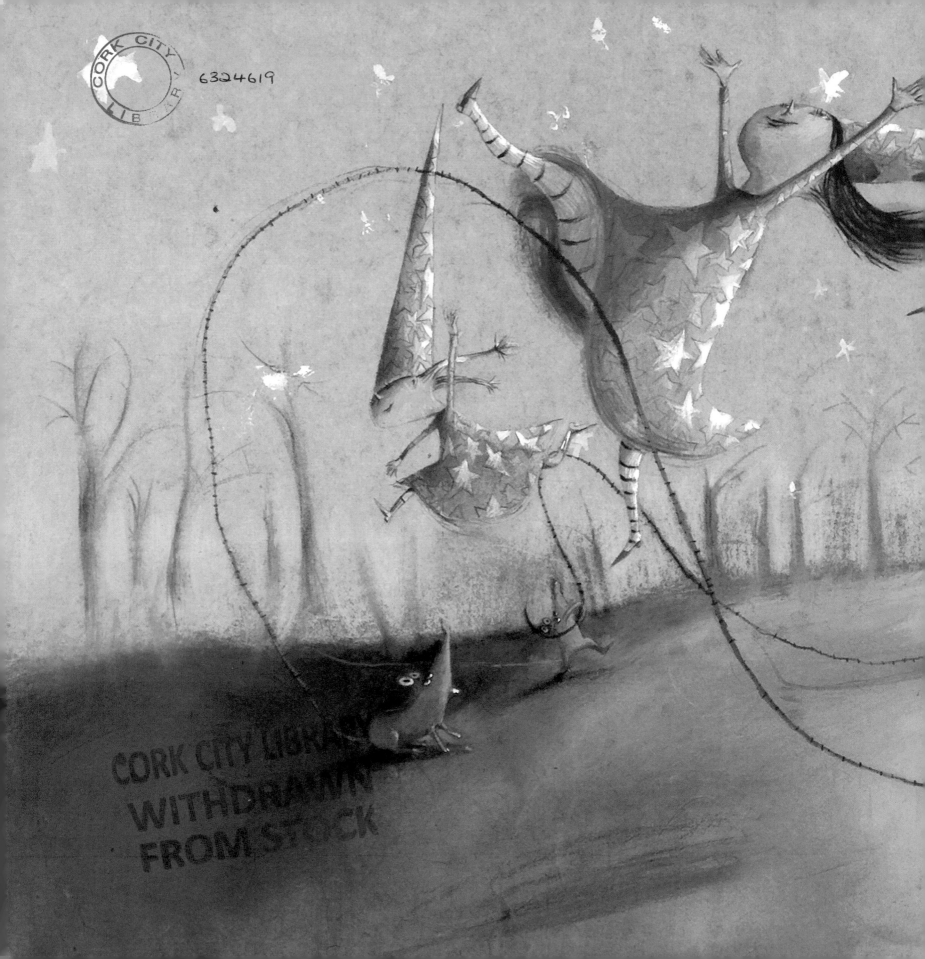

On starry nights, there are fairies in the woods.

And there
are witches…

Needless to say,
fairies and witches
are different.

And, needless to say,
they play different games.

Witches play witch games,
like turning princes into frogs.

And fairies play fairy games,
like turning frogs
back into princes.

And then there's Clotilda,
who hasn't any stars to be a fairy.

And her hat is too
pointed to be a witch.

And, needless to say,
if fairies and witches are so different…

...then Clotilda doesn't look
like either of them,
but a bit like both.

And that is why they never
let her play in their games.

So Clotilda has to
make do with
watching them
swinging on opposite
branches of the same tree.

Or dancing round a circle
in different directions.

Sometimes they ask her
to referee their races
of witches on broomsticks
against pumpkins
pulled by
mice.

Or to
referee
their battles of
crooked branches
against magic wands.

And then, one night,
they ask her to judge who it is,
witches or fairies,
that can build
the highest
pyramid,
up into
the sky.

When the last witch and
the last fairy are finally standing
on top of their pyramids,
Clotilda gives her verdict.

"They're exactly the same," says Clotilda.

"Impossible!"
they all shout.

"Climb our pyramid!"
the witches call out to her.

"No, climb ours!"
shout the fairies.

So Clotilda climbs
up the ladder made
of the feet and noses
of the witches and fairies.

"On our side!"
the fairies shout.

"No, ours!" shout the witches.

But Clotilda, who isn't a fairy
and who isn't a witch,
goes on up, up, up

and up some more.

Until she can see
straight into the
eyes of the stars.

She can touch the stars
with the tip of the hat
that is too pointed
to be a witch's hat…

… so pointed that it tickles the
stars, making them laugh,
laugh, laugh and laugh some more.

And the stars laugh so much,
that they can't hold on tight
to the sky anymore.

And so they fall.

They fall,
fall, fall and fall some more,
squashing the pointed hats
of the fairies and sticking
to the dresses of the witches.

And so, that night, in the woods,
you can't tell who is a witch,
and who is a fairy.

And that is because everyone,
starting from Clotilda right
at the top of the two pyramids,
and all of the witches and fairies,
all the way

down, down, down and down some more,
is happy being the same.

Ever since then, there are some nights
without stars, where the fairies
go on playing fairy games,
like making music with the
hats that they've managed
to straighten out.

And there are some
nights with stars,
where the witches
go on playing
witch games…

...like sticking the stars back
into the sky with glue.

But everyone's favourite game is to play
at being Clotilda, and being, like most of us,

a little bit

fairy

and a little

bit

witch!

A Nicoletta,

che non sa mai se è troppo fata o troppo strega.

Ma col pennello o senza, riesce sempre a fare magie!

This edition published in 2007
First published in 2006
by Meadowside Children's Books
185 Fleet Street, London, EC4A 2HS
www.meadowsidebooks.com

A CIP catalogue record for this book
is available from the British Library

ISBN 10 pbk 1-84539-288-4
ISBN 13 pbk 978-1-84539-288-8

10 9 8 7 6 5 4 3 2 1
Printed in Indonesia